Schott Saxophone Lounge

Jazz Standards

14 Most Beautiful Jazz Songs
Die 14 schönsten Jazz Songs

Arranged by / arrangiert von:
Dirko Juchem

Piano Score / Klaviersatz:
Harald Rutar

ED 21275
ISMN 979-0-001-18006-1
ISBN 978-3-7957-4628-5

Alto Saxophone
Altsaxophon

www.schott-music.com

Mainz · London · Berlin · Madrid · New York · Paris · Prague · Tokyo · Toronto

Contents / Inhalt

The CD was recorded and mastered at / die CD wurde aufgenommen & gemastered bei:
Krokodil Studios Holzappel, Germany + Pauler Acoustics Northeim, Germany

The musicians playing on this CD are / die Musiker auf der CD sind:
Dirko Juchem – Alto Saxophone
Harald Rutar – Piano / Klavier
Paul G. Ulrich – Bass
Bruce Busch – Drums / Schlagzeug

About the Songs

Killer Joe

The predominant characteristic of this jazz classic composed by Benny Golson is the urgently driving and constantly recurring bass line in the intro and A section. Besides the original version by the tenor saxophonist, it was the Big Band recording by Quincy Jones that made 'Killer Joe' famous.

In this song I use two techniques that may not be familiar to every saxophonist: In the solo (bars 41, 42 and 44) I play a 'fall off' at the end of the first note: this is a rapid downward glissando. The individual notes are not as important as the impression of 'slipping down' from the starting note. In bar 53 I use so-called 'ghost notes': these notes are played so softly that they can hardly be heard. Anyone who wants to find out more about these saxophone techniques will find precise explanations and exercises in the book 'Saxophone Sound' (SPL 1015, Schott Music).

What A Wonderful World

Composed especially for Louis Armstrong, this song was only recorded for the first time in 1967 and is thus relatively recent for a jazz classic. Besides performing well in the charts immediately after its release (e.g. No. 1 in the UK Charts), this lovely ballad came to international fame through its ironic use expressing anti-war sentiment in the film 'Good Morning, Vietnam'.

There are famous cover versions by Eva Cassidy, Celine Dion and Hawaiian singer Israel Kamakawiwo'ole, who accompanied 'What A Wonderful World' simply with his ukulele.

A Taste Of Honey

'A Taste Of Honey' was composed in 1960 by Bobby Scott, who initially recorded this song as a jazz ballad. The first cover versions soon appeared – first of all by The Beatles and shortly afterwards by the famous trumpeter Herb Alpert, who was awarded three Grammys for his instrumental version.

Of particular interest to saxophonists is the very cool version by Paul Desmond, who released this song on his legendary album 'Glad To Be Unhappy'.

Über die Songs

Killer Joe

Die extrem treibende und ständig wiederkehrende Basslinie im Intro und im A-Teil ist das typische Erkennungsmerkmal dieses von Benny Golson komponierten Jazzklassikers. Neben der Originalversion des Tenorsaxophonisten war es vor allem die Big Band-Aufnahme von Quincy Jones, die „Killer Joe" berühmt gemacht hat.

In diesem Song benutze ich zwei Techniken, die vielleicht nicht jedem Saxophonisten bekannt sind: Im Solo (Takt 41, 42, und 44) spiele ich am Ende der ersten Note ein „Fall Off". Dies ist ein schnell gespieltes, abfallendes Glissando. Hier kommt es weniger auf die einzelnen Töne an, sondern vielmehr dass es so klingt, als würde der Ton, von dem das Glissando ausgeht, „abschmieren". In Takt 53 verwende ich sogenannte „Ghostnotes". Diese Töne werden so leise gespielt, dass sie kaum richtig zu hören sind. Wer sich mit diesen Saxophontechniken intensiver beschäftigen möchte, findet genaue Erklärungen und Übungen in dem Buch „Saxophon Sound" (SPL 1015, Schott Music).

What A Wonderful World

Dieser speziell für Louis Armstrong komponierte Song wurde 1967 erstmals aufgenommen und ist damit für einen Jazzklassiker noch relativ jung. Neben guten Chartplatzierungen gleich nach der Veröffentlichung (z.B. Nr. 1 der Englischen Charts), gelangte diese wunderschöne Ballade durch die kontrastierende, kriegskritische Verwendung in dem Film „Good Morning, Vietnam" zu internationalem Ruhm. Berühmte Coverversionen gibt es von Eva Cassidy, Celine Dion und dem hawaiianischen Sängers Israel Kamakawiwo'ole, der „What A Wonderful World" nur mit seiner Ukulele begleitete.

A Taste Of Honey

Komponiert wurde „A Taste of Honey" 1960 von Bobby Scott, der diesen Song zunächst als Jazzballade eingesungen hatte. Schon bald gab es die ersten Coverversionen – allen voran von den Beatles und kurze Zeit später von dem berühmten Trompeter Herb Alpert, der für seine Instrumentalversion gleich mit 3 Grammys geehrt wurde.

Für uns Saxophonisten ist besonders die sehr coole Version von Paul Desmond interessant, der diesen Song auf seinem legendären Album „Glad To Be Unhappy" veröffentlicht hat.

Misty

For many jazz musicians 'Misty' is the quintessential jazz ballad. Erroll Garner was said to have composed this song on a plane, inspired by the weather conditions on a flight from San Francisco to Chicago. Besides very successful recordings by the composer, there have been innumerable versions by other jazz greats. It could be said that everyone who is anyone in jazz has performed this song at some time or another.

Work Song

With its soulful, bluesy melody 'Work Song' by Nat Adderley not only became a big jazz hit, but even found its way into rock and pop music in the 1960s. The best-known rock version is by the British band 'The Animals', while the best-known jazz versions are those by Cannonball Adderley and Nina Simone.

Bluessette

This jazz classic composed by the Belgian harmonica player Toots Thielemans is an inspired combination of elements of French accordion music with jazz and blues.
Thielemans did more than anyone else in jazz to establish the chromatic harmonica as a proper musical instrument, playing with international jazz greats such as Benny Goodman, George Shearing, Ella Fitzgerald and many others.

Honeysuckle Rose

This song is said to have been composed during a telephone call in which lyricist Andy Razaf read out the words he had already written to composer Fats Waller, who immediately set them to music on the piano and played the tune back over the telephone straight away. Its simple and harmonious chord structure made 'Honeysuckle Rose' one of the most popular songs at 'jam sessions' common at that time. Charlie Parker in particular seemed very taken with this sequence of chords, for he composed many songs of his own with harmonies based on 'Honeysuckle Rose'; the best-known of these is probably 'Scrabble From The Apple'.

Misty

Für viele Jazzmusiker ist „Misty" der Inbegriff der Jazzballade schlechthin. Angeblich hat Erroll Garner diesen Song im Flugzeug komponiert, angeregt durch die beeindruckenden Wetterverhältnisse während eines Fluges von San Francisco nach Chicago. Neben den sehr erfolgreichen Aufnahmen des Komponisten selbst gab es auch zahllose Versionen anderer Jazzgrößen. Man könnte eigentlich sagen, dass jeder, der im Jazz einen Namen hatte, diesen Song irgendwann einmal interpretiert hat.

Work Song

Mit seiner fast schon souligen und bluesigen Melodie wurde „Work Song" von Nat Adderley nicht nur im Jazz zu einem großen Hit, sondern hat in den 1960er Jahren auch Einzug in die Rock- und Popmusik gefunden. Die bekannteste Rockversion stammt von der britischen Band „The Animals". Die bekanntesten Jazzversionen stammen von Canonball Addreley und Nina Simone.

Bluessette

Dieser von dem belgischen Mundharmonikaspieler Toots Thielemans komponierte Jazzklassiker verbindet auf geniale Weise Elemente der französischen Musette-Musik mit Jazz und Blues. Thielemans etablierte wie kein anderer die chromatische Mundharmonika im Jazz als vollwertiges und eigenständiges Musikinstrument und spielte mit internationalen Jazzgrößen wie Benny Goodman, George Shearing, Ella Fitzgerald und vielen anderen.

Honeysuckle Rose

Angeblich wurde dieser Song während eines Telefonats komponiert, bei dem der Texter Andy Razaf seinen schon vorgefertigten Songtext dem Komponisten Fats Waller vorlas, der diesen sofort am Klavier vertonte und die Melodie direkt per Telefon zurück übermittelte. Die extrem stimmige und eingängige Akkordstruktur hat dazu geführt dass „Honeysuckle Rose" zu einem der beliebtesten Songs bei den damals üblichen „Jam Sessions" avancierte. Besonders Charlie Parker schien von dieser Akkordfolge sehr angetan gewesen zu sein, denn er hat viele eigene Songs komponiert, die in ihrer Harmonik auf „Honeysuckle Rose" basieren; der bekannteste dieser Parker-Titel dürfte „Scrabble From The Apple" sein.

Lullaby Of Birdland

George Shearing composed his most famous standard as a signature tune for the New York jazz club 'Birdland', whose name was intended to recall the famous saxophonist Charlie Parker, known as 'Bird'. Jazz bands appearing there would strike up 'Lullaby Of Birdland' every hour and the tune soon became very popular. The versions sung by Ella Fitzgerald and Sarah Vaughn helped to make 'Lullaby Of Birdland' an international hit. In recent times the version by the charismatic singer Amy Winehouse brought this classic back to modern audiences.

Willow Weep For Me

This song written by composer Ann Ronell draws its inherent tension from constant alternation between jazz ballad and Blues song. Though not composed as film music, 'Willow Weep For Me' reached a large audience through its use by the Marx Brothers in their film 'Love Letters'.

Part Of Me

This song truly in the style of the old swing standards is a tribute to jazz composer Gerald Marks.
Marks was famous above all for his composition 'All Of Me', which became one of the most often played jazz standards – performed in over a thousand different recordings by artists ranging from Louis Armstrong to Billie Holiday.

They Can't Take That Away From Me

This song was one of the great moments in the film 'Shall We Dance', when Ginger Rogers sang the tune – and Fred Astaire did not dance, for once, but just listened thoughtfully.
Here again, all the great jazz musicians have had a go at this song composed by George and Ira Gershwin, with cover versions recorded by artists such as Billie Holiday, Frank Sinatra, Charlie Parker, Robbie Williams and Rod Stewart.
One of the loveliest versions was recorded by Ella Fitzgerald and Louis Armstrong as a duet on their album 'Ella and Louis'.

Lullaby Of Birdland

George Shearing komponierte seinen berühmtesten Standard als Erkennungsmelodie für den New Yorker Jazzclub „Birdland", dessen Name an den berühmten Saxophonisten Charlie Parker erinnern sollte, der „Bird" genannt wurde. „Lullaby Of Birdland" wurde von den dort auftretenden Jazzbands einmal pro Stunde angestimmt und entwickelte sich dadurch sehr schnell zu einem echten Gassenhauer. Besonders die gesungenen Versionen von Ella Fitzgerald oder Sarah Vaughn verhalfen „Lullaby Of Birdland" zu seiner enormen internationalen Popularität. In neuerer Zeit hat die Version der charismatischen Sängerin Amy Winehouse diesen Klassiker wieder in Erinnerung gerufen.

Willow Weep For Me

Seine besondere Spannung erhält dieser von der Komponistin Ann Ronell geschriebene Song durch sein ständiges Schwanken zwischen Jazzballade und Bluessong. Zwar nicht als Filmmusik komponiert, fand „Willow Weep For Me" doch ein großes Publikum durch die Marx Brothers in ihrem Film „Love Letters" (deutsch: „Die Marx Brothers im Theater").

Part Of Me

Dieser ganz im Stil der alten Swingstandards komponierte Song ist eine Verbeugung vor dem Jazz-Komponisten Gerald Marks. Dieser wurde vor allem durch seine Komposition „All Of Me" berühmt, die mit über 1000 unterschiedlichen Einspielungen verschiedenster Künstler – von Louis Armstrong bis Billie Holiday – zu einem der meistgespielten Standards im Jazz gehört.

They Can't Take That Away From Me

Dieser Song war einer der großen Momente in dem Film „Shall We Dance" bei dem Ginger Rogers die Melodie sang - und Fred Astaire ausnahmsweise einmal nicht tanzte, sondern nur andächtig zuhörte. Und auch hier haben sich alle Größen der Jazzmusik an diesen von George und Ira Gershwin komponierten Song herangewagt und Coverversionen veröffentlicht, wie zum Beispiel Billie Holiday, Frank Sinatra, Charlie Parker, Robbie Williams und Rod Stewart. Eine der schönsten Versionen haben aber Ella Fitzgerald und Louis Armstrong im Duett auf ihrem gemeinsamen Album „Ella and Louis" eingesungen.

Chattanooga Choo Choo

This song was said to have been composed by Mack Gordon and Harry Warren during an actual train ride. 'Chattanooga Choo Choo' was made famous by the Glenn Miller Band, who played the song in the film 'Sun Valley Serenade'. There are cover versions by various Big Bands (e.g. Cab Calloway Orchestra), and even a Rock 'n' Roll version by Bill Haley & His Comets. In Germany this jazz classic was a great hit for Udo Lindenberg in 1983 with his song 'Special Train to Pankow'.

My Baby Just Cares For Me

Composed back in 1958 by Nina Simone for her first album 'Little Girl Blue', 'My Baby Just Cares For Me' became famous almost thirty years later – as the music to an advertisement for the perfume Chanel No. 5. The song was not released as a single until 1987 and the music video produced in the same year featured an animated cartoon with a band of cats and a black cat singer.
This wonderful song has seldom been covered, probably because it is so closely associated with Nina Simone's voice and her extraordinary piano playing style.

Billie Boy

Originally a typical American folksong, 'Billie Boy' found its way into jazz music through the brilliant up-tempo version by Red Garland on the album 'Milestones' by Miles Davis.
Besides various cover versions by other jazz musicians – all strongly influenced by the Garland version – saxophonist Nelson Rangell recorded an exciting new version for his album 'My New American Songbook Vol. 1'.

Chattanooga Choo Choo

Angeblich wurde der Song von Mack Gordon und Harry Warren tatsächlich während einer Zugfahrt komponiert. Berühmt wurde „Chattanooga Choo Choo" durch die Glenn Miller Band, die den Song in dem Film „Sun Valley Serenade" aufführte. Coverversionen gibt es von verschiedenen Big Bands (z. B. Cab Calloway Orchestra), aber auch in einer Rock 'n' Roll-Version von Bill Haley & His Comets. In Deutschland wurde dieser Jazzklassiker 1983 noch einmal zu einem großen Hit für Udo Lindenberg mit seinem „Sonderzug nach Pankow".

My Baby Just Cares For Me

Obwohl schon 1958 von Nina Simone für ihr erstes Album „Little Girl Blue" komponiert, wurde „My Baby Just Cares For Me" erst fast dreißig Jahre später berühmt – als Werbemusik für das Parfum „Chanel No. 5". So wurde dann auch die Single erst im Jahre 1987 veröffentlicht und das im gleichen Jahr produzierte Musikvideo zeigte einen animierten Trickfilm mit einer „Katzenband" und einer schwarzen Katzensängerin. Wahrscheinlich wurde dieser traumhafte Song deshalb kaum gecovert, weil er ganz extrem mit der Stimme Nina Simons, aber auch mit ihrem außergewöhnlichen Klavierspiel in Verbindung gebracht wird.

Billie Boy

Ursprünglich ein typischer „American Folksong", fand „Billie Boy" durch die geniale Uptempo-Version von Red Garland auf dem Album „Milestones" von Miles Davis Einzug in die Jazzmusik. Neben diversen Coverversionen anderer Jazzmusiker – die sich aber alle sehr stark an der Garland-Version orientierten – nahm der Saxophonist Nelson Rangell eine sehr spannende neue Version für sein Album „My New American Songbook Vol. 1" auf.

Song 01
Playback 15

Killer Joe

Shuffle / Swing
Musik und Text: Benny Golson
Arr.: Dirko Juchem
Intro
Bass:
5
A7 G9 A7 G9
9 A
A7 G9 A7 G9
Sax:
13
A7 G9 A7 G9
17 A2
A7 G9 A7 G9
21
A7 G9 A7 G9
25 B
C♯m7♭5 F♯7♭9 Cm7 F7
29
F♯7 F7 C♯m7 F♯7
33 A3
A7 G9 A7 G9
37
A7 G9 A7 G9

Solo
41 A7 G9 A7 G9
45 A7 G9 A7 G9
A2
49 A7 G9 A7 G9
53 A7 G9 A7 G9
B
57 C♯m7♭5 F♯7♭9 Cm7 F7
61 F♯7 F7 C♯m7 F♯7
A3
65 A7 G9 A7 G9
69 A7 G9 A7 G9
73 A7 G9 A7 G9 A7

What A Wonderful World

Song 02
Playback 16

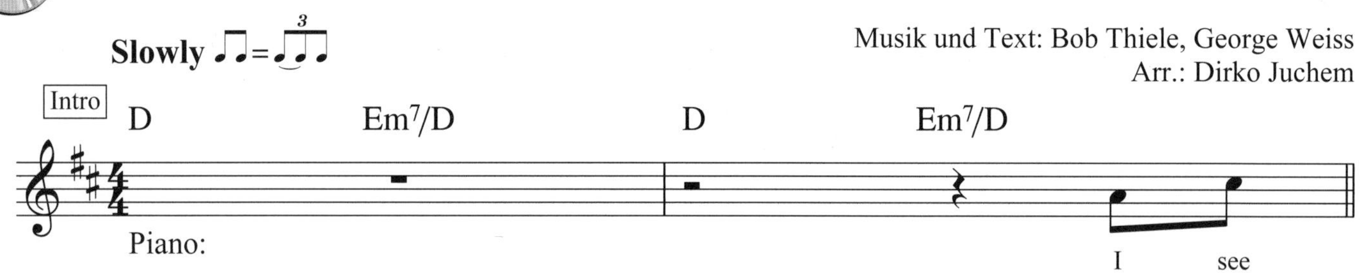

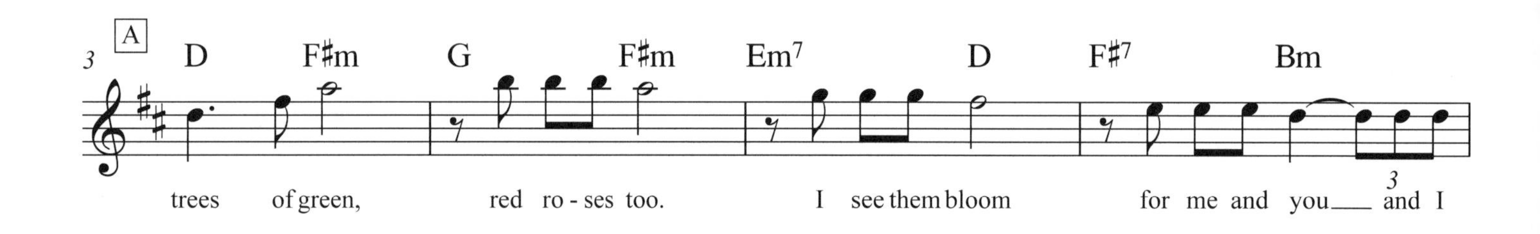

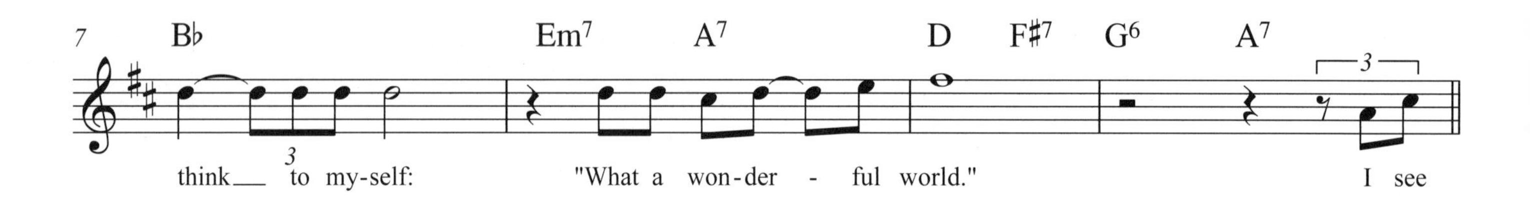

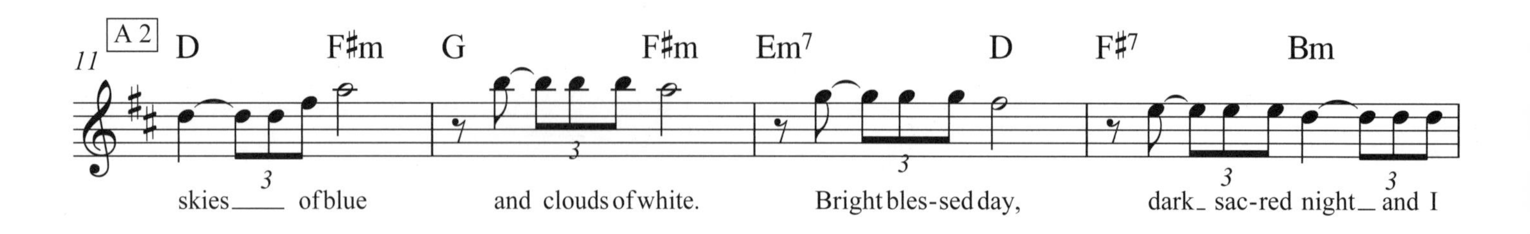

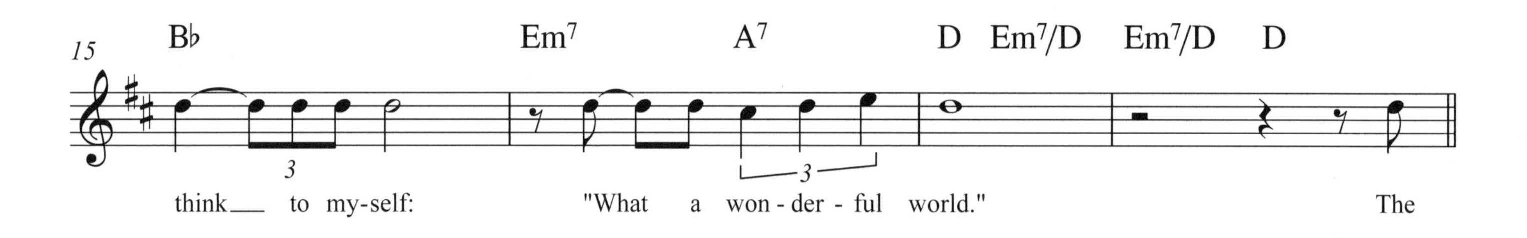

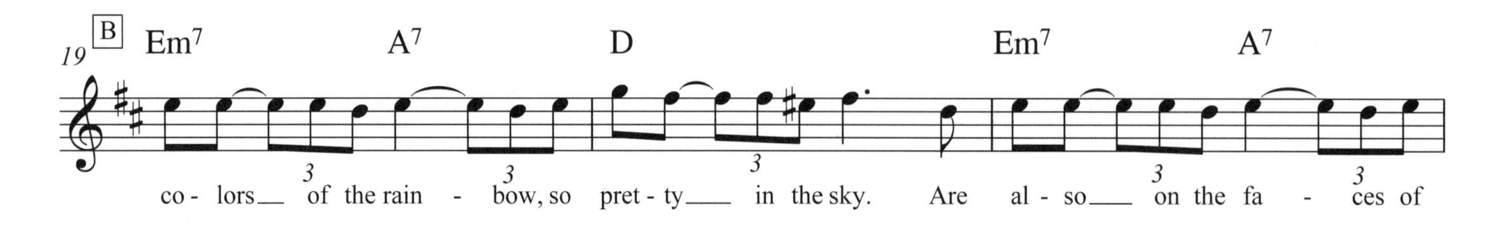

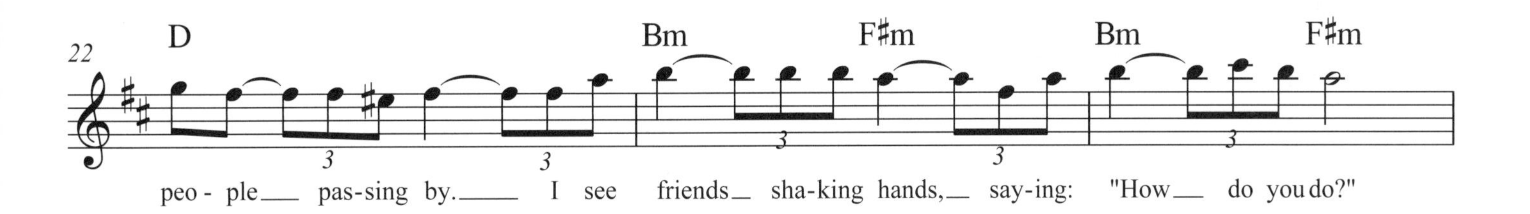
22
D
Bm
F♯m
Bm
F♯m
peo - ple pas-sing by. I see friends sha-king hands, say-ing: "How do you do?"

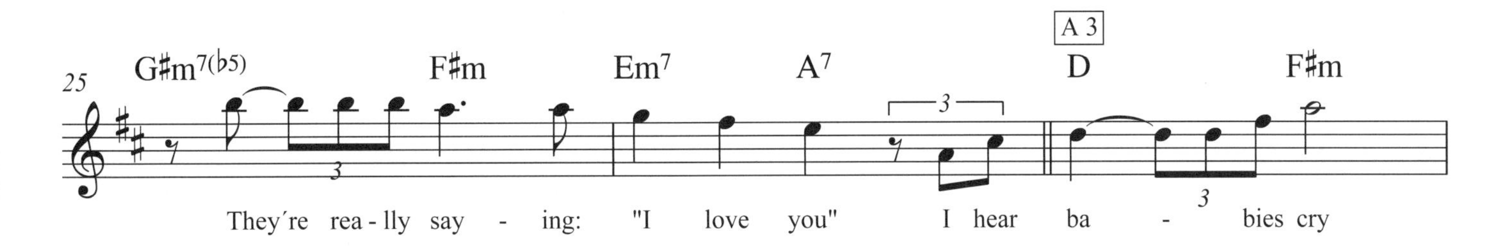
25
A 3
G♯m7(♭5)
F♯m
Em7
A7
D
F♯m
They´re rea - lly say - ing: "I love you" I hear ba - bies cry

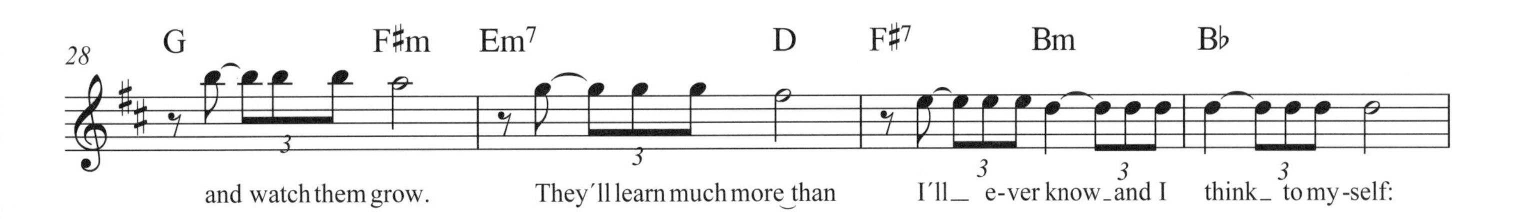
28
G
F♯m
Em7
D
F♯7
Bm
B♭
and watch them grow. They´ll learn much more than I´ll e-ver know and I think to my-self:

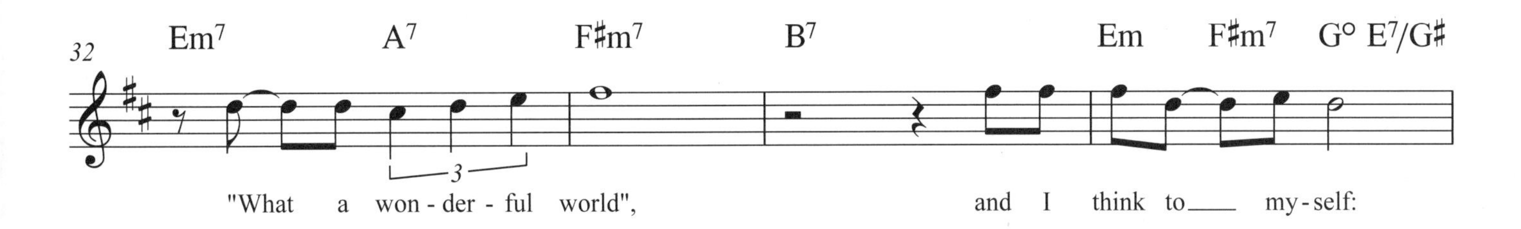
32
Em7
A7
F♯m7
B7
Em
F♯m7
G° E7/G♯
"What a won - der - ful world", and I think to my-self:

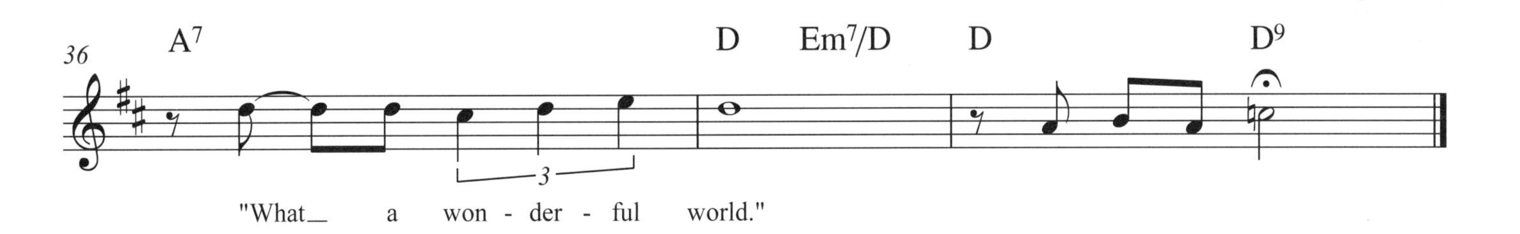
36
A7
D
Em7/D
D
D9
"What a won - der - ful world."

Song 03
Playback 17
A Taste Of Honey
Swing Waltz
Musik: Bobby Scott / Originaltext: Ric Marlow
Arr.: Dirko Juchem
Intro
Dm Dm△/C♯ Dm7/C G/B A7(♯9)
Piano:
A
Dm Dm△ Dm7 G7/B
Winds may blow over the i - - cy sea,
Dm Dm△ Dm7 G7/B
I'll take with me the warmth of thee. A taste of
E♭maj7 B♭maj7 C Dm/A A7(♯9)
hon - ey, a taste much sweeter than wine.
B
Dm7 G7 Dm7/F G7
I will re - turn, I'll re - turn I'll
B♭ C Dm A7(♯9)
come back for honey and you.
Solo
Dm Dm△ Dm7 G7
Dm Dm△ Dm7 G

35
Ebmaj7
Bbmaj7
C
B
39
Dm
Dm
Dm7
G7
43
Dm7
G7
Bb
C
A
47
Dm
A7(#9)
Dm
DmΔ
I'll leave be - hind my
51
Dm7
G7/B
Dm
DmΔ
heart to wear and may it ever re -
55
Dm7
G7/B
3
Ebmaj7
- mind you of a taste of hon - ey, a
59
Bbmaj7
C
Dm/A
A7(#9)
taste much sweet - er than wine.
63
Dm7
G7
Dm7/F
G7
I will re - turn, I'll re - turn. I'll
67
Bb
C
Dm
A7(#9)
Dm
come back for honey and you.

Misty

Musik: Erroll Garner, Text: Johnny Burke
Arr.: Dirko Juchem

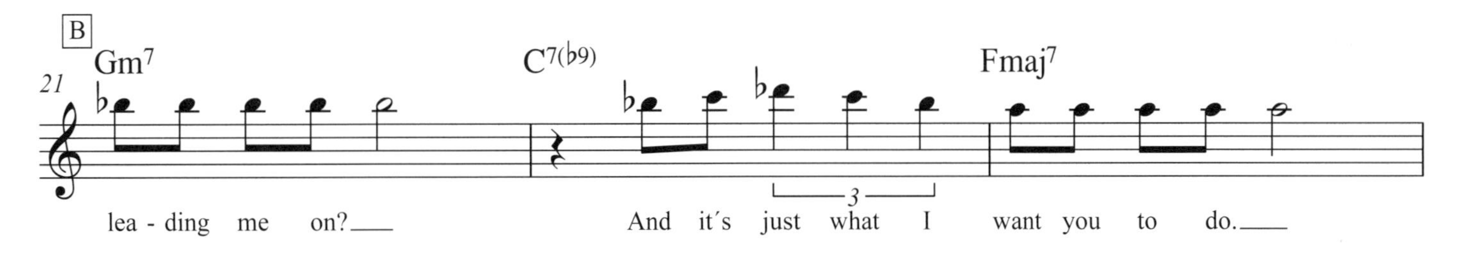
B
21
Gm7
C7(♭9)
Fmaj7
lea - ding me on?
And it´s just what I want you to do.

24
F♯m7
B7
D7
Don´t you no - tice how hope - less - ly I´m lost?
That´s why I´m fol - low - ing

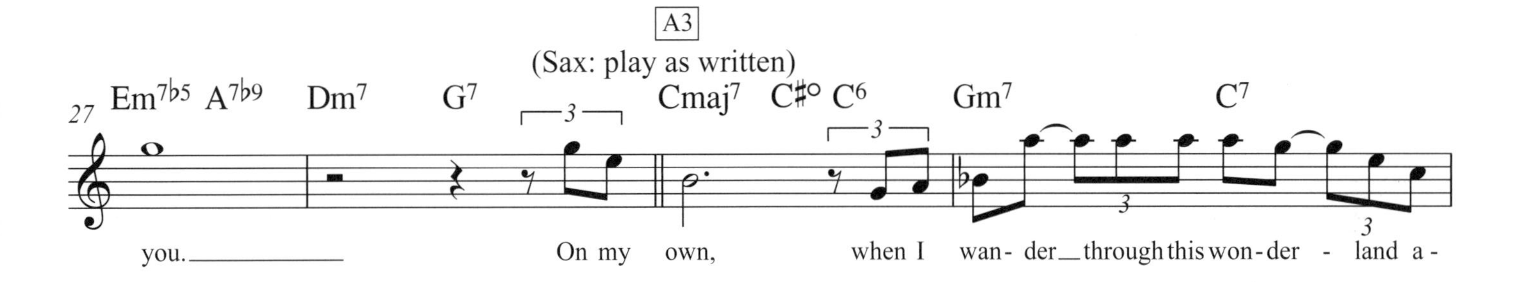
A3
(Sax: play as written)
27
Em7♭5
A7♭9
Dm7
G7
Cmaj7
C♯o
C6
Gm7
C7
you.
On my own, when I wan- der through this won - der - land a -

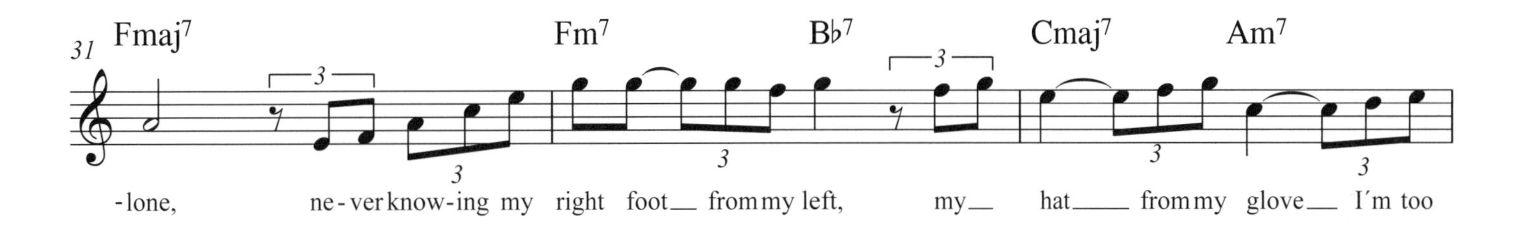
31
Fmaj7
Fm7
B♭7
Cmaj7
Am7
- lone, ne - ver know - ing my right foot from my left, my hat from my glove I´m too

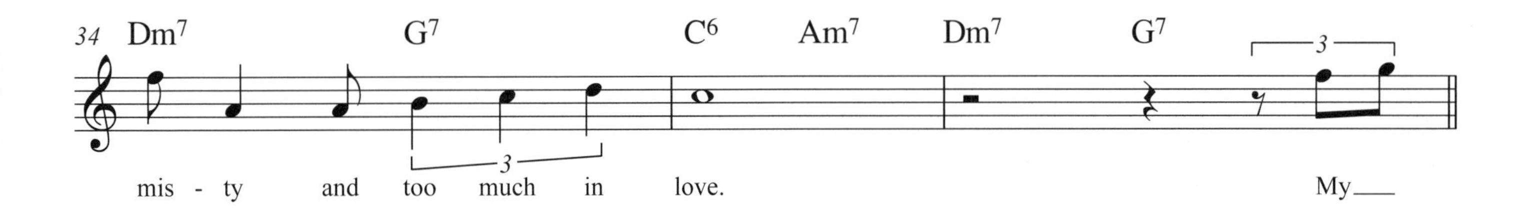
34
Dm7
G7
C6
Am7
Dm7
G7
mis - ty and too much in love.
My

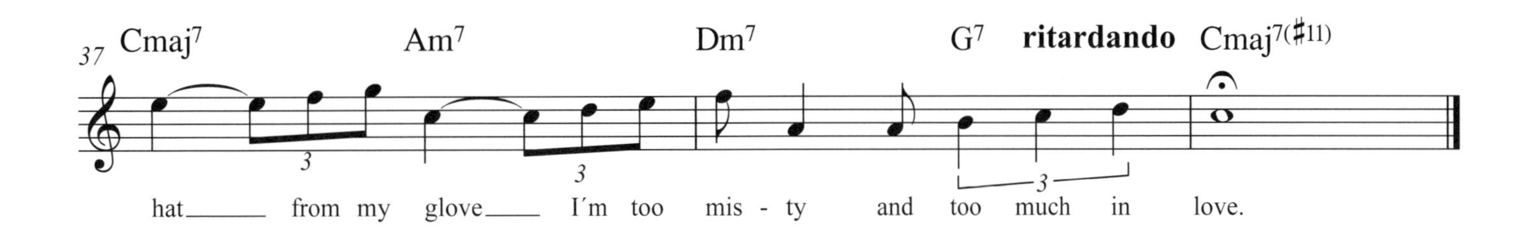
37
Cmaj7
Am7
Dm7
G7
ritardando
Cmaj7(♯11)
hat from my glove I´m too mis - ty and too much in love.

Work Song

Musik: Nat Adderly, Text: Oscar Brown Jr
Arr.: Dirko Juchem

Solo
37
Dm7
41
Dm7
A7
45
Dm7
49
D7
G7
B♭7
A7
Dm
Chorus 3
53
Dm7
57
Dm7
A7
61
Dm7
3
65
D7
G7
B♭7
A7
Dm
69
D7
G7
B♭7
A7
Dm
Slowly (Half Time)
73
D7
G7
B♭7
A7
Dm

Bluesette

Musik: Jean Thielemans
Arr.: Dirko Juchem

42 B♭maj7 B♭m7 E♭7
46 A♭maj7 Am7♭5 D7
50 Bm7 B♭7 Am7 D7
Solo
54 Gmaj7 F♯m7♭5 B7♭9
58 Em7 A7 Dm7 G7
62 Cmaj7 Cm7 F7
66 B♭maj7 B♭m7 E♭7
70 A♭maj7 Am7♭5 D7
74 Bm7 B♭7 Am7 D7
D.S. al Coda
78 Bm7 B♭7 Am7 D7 G
play 3 times

Song 07
Playback 21
Honeysuckle Rose
Musik: Thomas Fats Waller, Text: Andy Razaf
Arr.: Dirko Juchem
Medium Swing
Intro
F♯m7 B7 Fm7 B♭7 Em7 A7 D B7(♭9)
Piano:
A
Em7 A7 Em7 A7 Em7 A7 Em7 A7
Ev-`ry ho-ney-bee fills with jea-lou-sy when they see you out with me, I don´t blame them
D Bm7 Em7 A7 D F♯m7(♭5) B7♭9
good - ness knows, Ho - ney - suck - le Rose.
A2
Em7 A7 Em7 A7 Em7 A7 Em7 A7
When you´re pas-ing by, flo-wers droop and sigh and I know the rea - son why, you´re much swee-ter
D Bm7 Em7 A7 D A7 D
good - ness knows, Ho - ney-suck - le Rose.
B
Am7 D7 G
Don´t buy su - gar, you just have to touch my cup.
E7 A7
You´re my su - gar, it´s sweet when you stir it up.
A3
Em7 A7 Em7 A7 Em7 A7 Em7 A7
When I´m ta-king sips from your tas - ty lips, seems the ho-ney fair - ly drips, your con-fec-tion

33 D Bm7 Em7 A7 D F♯m7(♭5) B7♭9
good - ness knows, Ho - ney - suck - le Rose.
Solo
37 Em7 A7 Em7 A7 Em7 A7 Em7 A7
41 D Bm7 Em7 A7 D F♯m7(♭5) B7♭9
A2
45 Em7 A7 Em7 A7 Em7 A7 Em7 A7
3
3
3
49 D Bm7 Em7 A7 D A7 D
B
53 Am7 D7 G
57 E7 A7
A3
61 Em7 A7 Em7 A7 Em7 A7 Em7 A7
When I´m ta-king sips from your tas - ty lips, seems the ho-ney fair - ly drips, your con-fec-tion
65 D Bm7 Em7 A7 D Bm7 Em7 A7
good-ness knows, Ho - ney-suck - le Rose. Ho - ney-suck - le
69 D Bm7 Em7 A7 D
Rose. Ho-ney-suck - le Rose.

Lullaby Of Birdland

Fmaj7 Dm7 Gm7 C7(♭9) Fmaj7 C7(♭9) Fmaj7 A7
- ing high in Bird - land high in the sky up a - bove, we're in love.
Solo
Dm E7 A7 Dm Gm7 C7
Fmaj7 Dm7 Gm7 C7 Fmaj7 B♭7 A7
A2
Dm E7 A7 Dm Gm7 C7
Fmaj7 Dm7 Gm7 C7 Fmaj7 C7(♭9) Fmaj7 A7/E
B
D7 Gm7 Gm7 C7 Fmaj7
And there's a weepy old wil - low, he real - ly knows how to cry.
D7 Gm7 Gm7 C7 Fmaj7 A7
That's how I'd cry in my pil - low, if you should tell me fare - well and good-bye.
A2
Dm E7 A7 Dm Gm7 C7
Lul - la - by of Bird-land whis - per low, kiss me sweet, and we'll go. Fly-
Fmaj7 Dm7 Gm7 C7 Fmaj7 C7(♭9) Fmaj7
- ing high in Bird-land, high in the sky up a- bove, we're in love.

Willow Weep For Me

Musik & Text: Ann Ronell
Arr.: Dirko Juchem

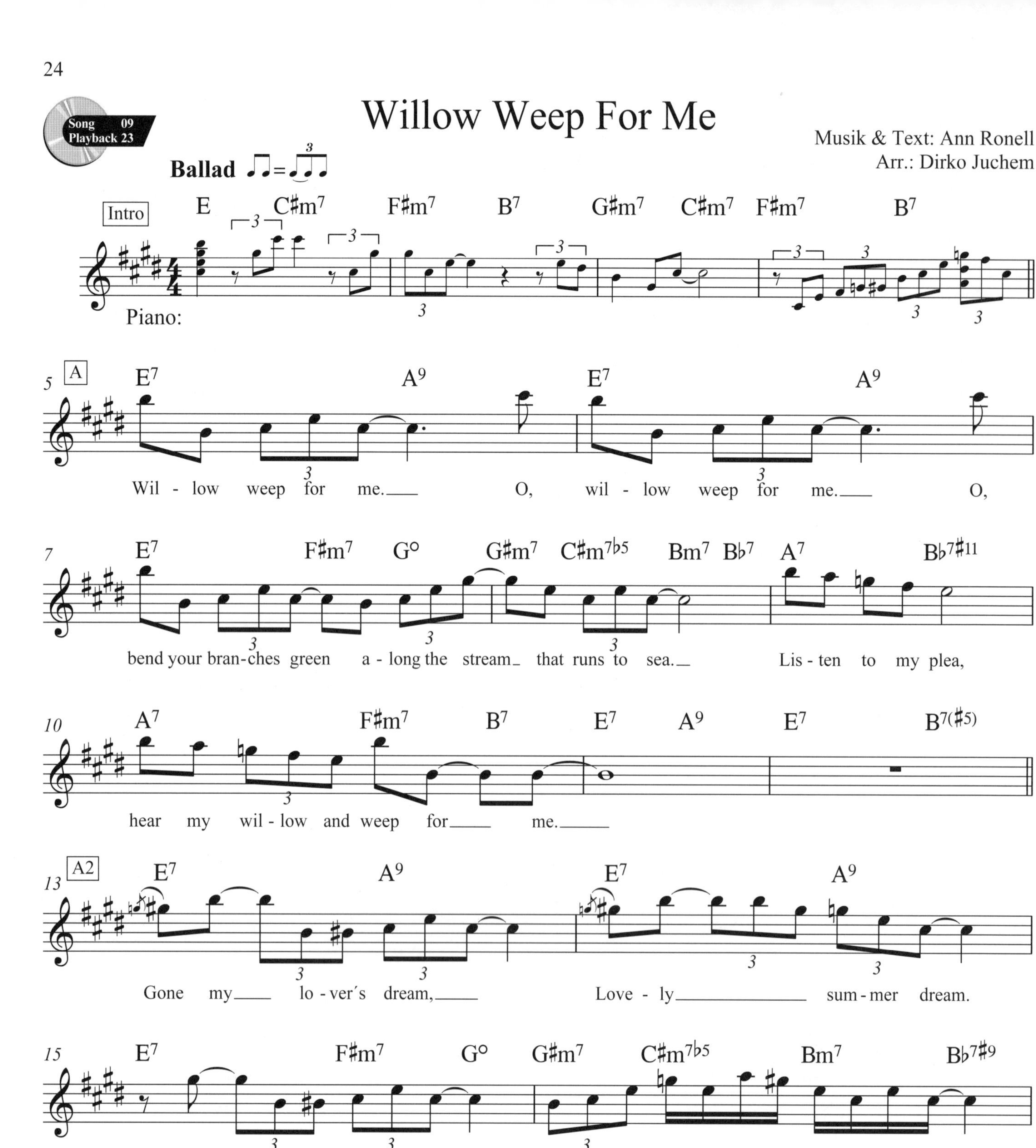

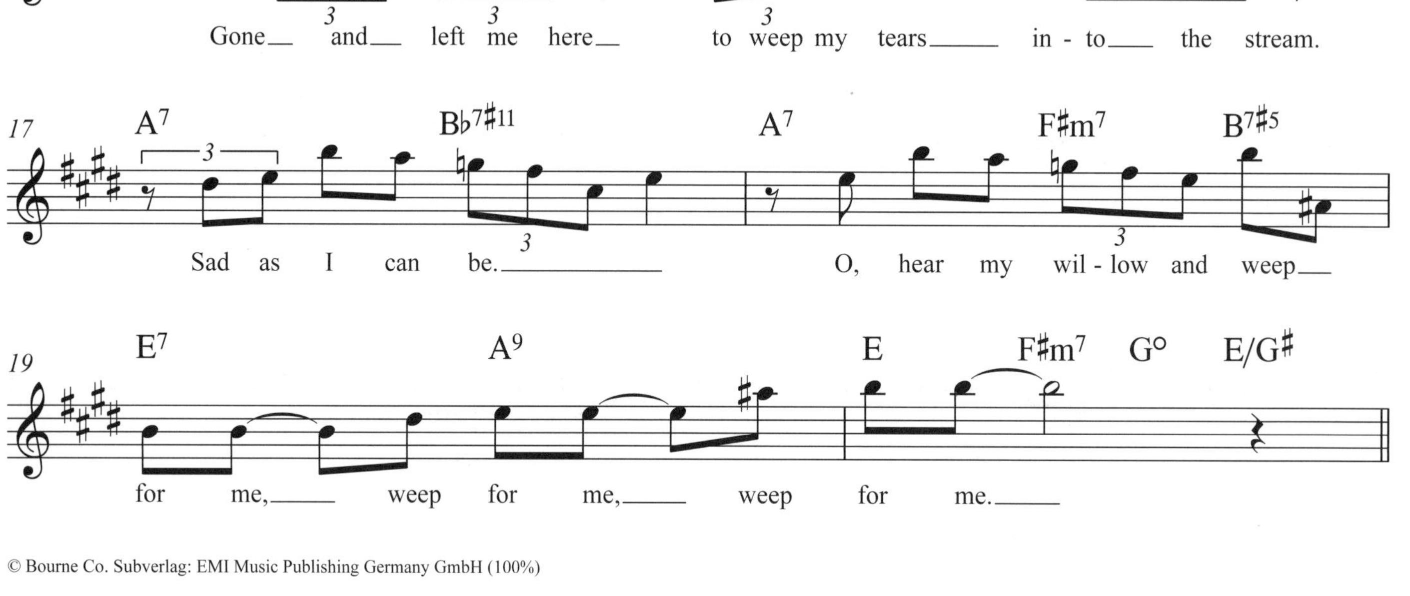

B
Am Am/G F♯m7♭5 B7♭9 Em E7
Whis - per to the wind and say that love has sinned. And
Em7 A7 Dm7 G7 Cm7 F7 Bm7 E7
left my heart a - brea - king and ma - king a moan.
Am Am/G F♯m7♭5 B7♭9 Em E7
Mur - mur to the night to hide its star - ry light. So
Em7 A7 Dm7 G7 Cm7 F7 F♯m7 B7
none will see me sigh - ing and cry - ing all a - lone.
A
E7 A9 E7 A9
Wee - ping wil - low tree. O, weep in sym - pa - thy. O,
E7 F♯m7 G° G♯m7 C♯m7(♭5) Bm7 B♭7
bend your bran - ches down a - long the ground and co - ver me.
A7 B♭7♯11 A7 F♯m7 B7
When the sha - dows fall, hear my wil - low and weep for me.
E7 A9 E7 A9 E7 A9 E7 B9 E13
Wil - low weep for me.

Part Of Me

Medium Swing

Dirko Juchem

Solo
Amaj7
C#7
F#7
Bm7
C#7
F#m7
B7
Bm7
E7
B
Amaj7
C#7
F#7
Bm7
D
Dm
Amaj7
F#7
Bm7
E7
Bm7
E7
Bm7
E7
A
Bm7/E
C°/E
A6

They Can´t Take That Away From Me

Musik und Text: George Gershwin, Ira Gershwin
Arr.: Dirko Juchem

Solo
me.
A 2
We may
B
ne - ver, ne- ver, ne - ver, ne-ver meet a-gain on the bum-py road to love. Still I
al- ways, al - ways keep the mem´-ry of. The way you hold your
A 2
knife, the way we danced till three. The way you´ve changed my life,
no, no, they can´t take that a-way from me. No, they can´t take that a - way from
me. No, they can´t take that a - way from me.

Chattanooga Choo Choo

Musik: Harry Warren, Text: Mack Gordon
Arr.: Dirko Juchem

34
D6/A B7 E7♭9 E7♭9 A7 D6 E
got - ta keep it rol - ling. Woo woo Chat - ta - noo - ga, there you are.
A3
37
A6 A7 D D♯o
She´s gon - na cry, un - til I tell her that I´ll ne - ver roam, So
41
A F♯m7 Bm7 E7 A F♯m7 E7
Chat - ta - noo - ga Choo Choo Won´t you choo choo me home?
Intro
4
A
49
A6
Par - don me boy, is that the Chat - ta - noo - ga Choo Choo? Track twen - ty nine
53
Bm7 E7 A E7
boy you can give me a shine.
A3
57
A6 A7 D6 D♯o
She´s gon - na cry, un - til I tell her that I´ll ne - ver roam, So
61
A6 F♯m7 Bm7 E7 A D7 C♯7 C7 B7 E7
Chat - ta - noo - ga Choo Choo Won´t you choo choo me home? So
65
A6 F♯m7 Bm7 E7 A D7 C♯7 C7 B7 E7
Chat - ta - noo - ga Choo Choo Won´t you choo choo me home? So
69
A F♯m7 Bm7 E7 A A13
Chat - ta - noo - ga Choo Choo Won´t you choo choo me home?

My Baby Just Cares For Me

(16 Takte Pause zur CD / 32 Takte Pause mit Klavierbegleitung)
(CD contains 16 bars, piano part 32 bars of piano solo)

53
A
G6
Am7
D7sus4
G6
Am7
D7sus4
Ba-by, my ba-by don´t care for shows and he don´t e-ven care for clothes.
57
G6
Am7
D7
He cares for me.
61
B
B7
Em7
My ba - by don´t care for cars and ra - ces.
65
A7
D7
My ba - by don´t care for, he don´t care for hot town pla - ces.
69
A
G6
Am7
D7sus4
G6
Am7
D7sus4
Liz Tay-lor is not his style and e - ven Li - ber - a - ce´s smile
73
G6
C6
is some - thing he can´t see, is some-thing he can´t see.
77
C
C6
F#
G
F
E7
I won-der what´s wrong with ba - - - by?
81
Am7
D7
Bm7
Em7
My ba - by just cares for, my ba - by just cares for.
85
Am7
D7
G6
My ba-by just cares for me.

Song 14
Playback 28
Billy Boy
Up-Tempo
Trad.
Arr.: Dirko Juchem
Intro
Piano:
Sax:
A
Amaj7 Bm7 E7(b9) Amaj7 F#m7 Bm7 E7(b9)
Amaj7 C#m7(b5) F#7b9 Bm7 F#7b9
Bm7 Bm7 E7 A7 D7
Bm7 E7 Amaj7 F#m7 Bm7 E7
A2
Amaj7 Bm7 E7(b9) Amaj7 F#7 Bm7 E7b9
Amaj7 C#m7(b5) F#7b9 Bm7 F#7b9
Bm7 Bm7 E7 A7 D7
Bm7 E7 Amaj7 F#m7 Fm7 Bb7

B
A Bm7 E7 Amaj7 F♯7 Bm7 E7
Piano (Sax play ad lib.):
Sax:
D♯m7(♭5) G♯7 C♯m7(♭5) F♯7 Bm7(♭5) E Bm E7
C
Amaj7 Bm7 E7(♭9) Amaj7 F♯m7 Bm7 E7
Amaj7 C♯m7(♭5) F♯7♭9 Bm7 F♯7♭9
Bm7 E7 A7 D7
Bm7 E7 Amaj7 F♯m7 Fm7 B♭7
B
A Bm7 E7 Amaj7 F♯7 Bm7 E7
Piano (Sax play ad lib.):
Sax:
D♯m7(♭5) G♯7 C♯m7(♭5) F♯7 Bm7(♭5) E7 Bm E7
D.S. al Coda
D7 Bm7 E7 Amaj7 F♯7 D7
Slowly
C♯m7 F7/C Bm7 B♭13 E7 Bm7/E E7 Amaj7 G13 G/F B/A